COWBOYS

GLEN ROUNDS

HOLIDAY HOUSE ~ NEW YORK

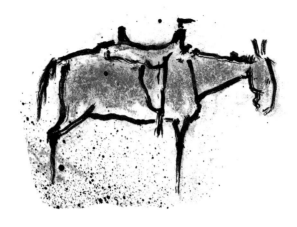

Library of Congress Cataloging-in-Publication Data

Rounds, Glen.
Cowboys / by Glen Rounds. — 1st ed.
p.   cm.
Summary: Follows a cowboy from sunup to bedtime as he rounds
up cattle, kills a rattlesnake, and plays cards in the
bunkhouse after dinner.
ISBN 0-8234-0867-1
[1. Cowboys—Fiction.]   I. Title.
PZ7.R761Co   1991
[E]—dc20
90-46501   CIP   AC
ISBN 0-8234-0867-1

COWBOYS

THE RANCHER HIRES
COWBOYS TO RIDE THE
RANGE FOR HIM ~

IN THE BUNKHOUSE AFTER
SUPPER, THE COWBOYS PLAY
CARDS OR READ WESTERN
STORY MAGAZINES ⌐

A COWBOY'S FIRST CHORE
AFTER BREAKFAST IS TO
CATCH AND SADDLE A HORSE —

BUT SOMETIMES THAT'S EASIER SAID THAN DONE!

AND EVEN AFTER HE'S IN
THE SADDLE, THE COWBOY'S
TROUBLES MAY NOT BE OVER~

WHEN A COWBOY IS
THROWN, HE'S EXPECTED
TO CLIMB RIGHT BACK
ONTO HIS HORSE AGAIN ~

BY SUNUP ALL OF THE
COWBOYS ARE READY
TO RIDE OUT ONTO
THE RANGE ~

THEY WILL RIDE INTO
GULLIES AND THICKETS
AND ACROSS WIDE FLATS,
LOOKING FOR STRAY CATTLE﹘

A COWBOY FINDS A COW
BOGGED DOWN IN A MUDDY
WATER HOLE AND USES HIS
ROPE TO PULL HER OUT~

A STEER TRYING TO GET
AWAY HAS TO BE ROPED
AND BROUGHT BACK ~

THIS RATTLESNAKE'S SKIN
WILL MAKE THE COWBOY A
FANCY BELT AND HAT BAND ~

LATE IN THE AFTERNOON
A SUDDEN FLASH OF LIGHTNING
AND ROLL OF THUNDER SET
THE HERD RUNNING IN A
WILD STAMPEDE!!

BUT THE COWBOYS SOON
ROUND UP THE SCATTERED
CATTLE AND DRIVE THEM
INTO THE RANCH CORRALS
JUST AT SUNDOWN...

AFTER THEY UNSADDLE
THEIR HORSES AND TURN
THEM LOOSE, THE TIRED
COWBOYS GO TO THE
BUNKHOUSE TO WAIT FOR
THE SUPPER BELL - -